A BEARY HAPPILY
EVER AFTER

Bear Clan, 6

JENIKA SNOW

A BEARy Happily Ever After

Damon

An alpha, bear-shifting virgin who was saving himself for his mate.

That's what I was. And I was fine with that, because saving myself for the one female who was meant to be mine was the only thing I ever wanted.

A lone bear without a mate was a depressing thing. And even though I knew she was out there—the other half to my soul—I was beginning to think there was no happily ever after for me.

Until I saw another male lusting after her. There was no way I could control myself. She was mine, and if that meant kicking the ass of the man who wanted her… then so be it.

Rue would be mine.

Rue

It started with a swim in the lake, and then suddenly there was a possessive bear shifter tackling my friend to the ground for touching my hair. It ended with me being pressed up against a tree, staring into the dark eyes of a feral man who claimed I was his mate… that he wouldn't stop until I was his, until I was *marked* as his.

And as much as I knew being mated to Damon meant my life would be forever changed, knowing he would never let me go, would scare off any male who even looked in my direction, all I wanted was to be with him.

All I wanted was to wear his mark.

Chapter One

Damon

I had to get out of there, away from my brothers and their mates, away from the feeling of being an outcast. It was as if I'd never find what I was missing and forever live my life on the outside looking in.

It was this constant hollowness inside me, this hole that would never be filled until I found her.

My mate.

She was out there somewhere, but for all I knew, she could've been on a different continent.

I felt distant, detached. I was getting older, my life continuing to move forward even though I felt like I was being pushed back, further and further, until I'd never catch up.

I continued through the woods on the trail my brothers and I had made years ago. We didn't need hiking paths, not when our bears trampled through everything. The only thing they were mindful of was being free. But we'd thought of the future, of our mates and children, of family walks and picnics.

And all my brothers had that now.

All of them, but not me.

I lifted my hand and rubbed my palm over the center of my chest, right over my heart, right where the hole was, where there was this painful reminder. All I wanted was to find my mate, to feel my happiness. All I needed was that realization that I wasn't actually alone in life.

I shoved my hands in my pockets, staying in my human form even though my bear wanted out, wanted to run free and get rid of some of this aggression and frustration.

I liked leisurely walking as a human, taking in the sights and smells, feeling the sun warm my skin. It was the little things I appreciated, that I didn't take for granted.

I was at the edge of our property, the lake not too far from where I was right now. The path had since ended, my boots crunching along the rocky, uneven forest terrain.

It was another ten-minute walk before I found myself getting closer to the lake. I inhaled deeply, smelling the scent of the fish in the water, the birds up in the trees.

I heard the sound of a masculine voice, of splashing. I didn't know why I followed that noise, stopped, and looked at where I saw the man wading in the water. He was facing off to the side, an area where the trees obscured my view, laughing and splashing water in that direction. I moved to the side so I could get a better look at who he was speaking to, not sure why I gave a fuck.

I should've kept walking, minded my own business. But the first thing I saw was the fall of long dark hair. My heart lurched in my chest when she turned around and started swimming toward the shore, laughing as the man continued to splash her.

The sound of her voice was the sweetest thing I'd ever heard.

And when she climbed out of the lake, the water dripping down her lean yet curvy body, I felt my cock instantly harden. It pressed against the fly of my jeans, demanding to get out. My canines lengthened, my nails turning into claws. My grizzly pushed forward, my skin stretching, my muscles thickening.

My mate.

Mine.

She was there, just down on the bank, close enough I could smell the scent of lemons and gardenia surrounding her. Everything happened in slow motion, time standing still as everything fell into place.

The man crawled out of the lake, his focus trained on her. I inhaled deeply, the wind coming upwind and letting me take in every scent. A low growl left me. I smelled desire from him. For her.

But from her... from her, I only scented distance. Good, she didn't want him. If she had, then that would've caused complications. Hell, him wanting her already caused problems.

And then as I watched him reach out, trying to push a strand of hair off her shoulder, every territorial and possessive instinct in my body rose up. I was jealous, fierce in that moment. No other male would touch her. No other male would even think about having her.

She was mine.

And that's all I thought about as I charged forward, about to make my claim known.

Chapter Two

Rue

I took a step back so Ronnie didn't touch my hair again. I knew he had a thing for me, and for as many hints as I'd given him over the years that I just wasn't interested, that I only saw him as a family friend, he was either blind, thick-headed, or didn't care, because he persisted.

But he had been in my life forever, and I didn't want to lose that by being a cold bitch and shutting him out. He was a good friend, had been there for me through hard and good times. He was a shoulder to cry on, an ear that listened to every-thing I had to say. He just needed to find someone who could complete him.

But that someone wasn't me.

"We should go into town and get dinner or a drink," Ronnie said as he grabbed one of the towels we'd brought with us and started drying off his hair.

I grabbed the other one and did the same. Our family had gotten together for the weekend to camp not too far from the lake. And after my mother insisted we go for a dip in the water while they cooked dinner, Ronnie all but pulling me along, here we were, soaking wet and knowing that this probably meant more to him than it ever would to me.

"Listen, Ronnie," I said, about to tell him again that there would be nothing between us, hopefully for the last time, that I just saw us as friends. Because I knew if I agreed to go out to dinner and drinks tonight, it would be more than what it really was. I had tried to nip this in the bud more times than I could count, but it seemed like it wasn't getting through to him. It seemed like me telling him what a good friend he was, how I saw him as my brother, fell on deaf ears.

But before I could start speaking again, I heard something coming closer, this thumping and pounding that seemed to vibrate the very ground I stood on. Was it a stampede of wild animals? It sure as hell sounded that way.

I turned my head to my left to where the noise was coming from and at first didn't see anything. I glanced at Ronnie and saw he was looking in the same direction I had been, hearing the same thing.

"What is that?" I turned back and faced the sound, and after only a second, I saw a man barreling toward us. I knitted my brows in confusion… and a little bit of surprise and fear.

The expression on this stranger's face was fierce, focused right on Ronnie. He looked angry, enraged. He was big, lean with muscles stacked under his golden skin. It was as if everything happened in slow motion as I stared at him, took in his fierceness. Short dark hair, square cut jaw. His lips were full, his nose straight. His dark eyebrows were knitted low, and his equally dark eyes were hard set…

On Ronnie.

"What the fuck?" Ronnie murmured, but I couldn't take my focus off the man coming at us. "Who is that?"

I shook my head, although I felt like that was a lie.

I know him. But I don't. What's going on?

7

Those words played through my mind over and over again. I didn't know who this man was, had never seen him before, but I felt his anger, his… possessiveness.

The latter toward me.

"What's going on?" I whispered, not even sure anyone but myself had heard. And as the man kept coming toward us… toward Ronnie, all I could do was stand there, watch him as he slammed into Ronnie with so much force he was propelled backward.

I cried out involuntarily and covered my mouth with my hand, feeling my eyes widen. Ronnie grunted out in pain as he slammed hard against the ground. The man who'd been coming at us like a wild animal was now on top on Ronnie, his fist slamming into his gut, the side of his face. Everywhere.

I snapped to attention, ran over to them, and grabbed the stranger's bulky, muscular arm. It was like concrete under my touch, turning me on, heating me from the inside out.

And that had everything in me stilling. That one touch. I felt something in him change as well, as he froze, stopped beating on Ronnie, and slowly turned his head to look at me. Our gazes locked, his dark eyes penetrating mine, the world coming into focus, everything seeming... like it finally fit.

I stumbled back, my hand feeling on fire. I looked down at it, expecting to see flames. It wasn't painful, but the feeling consumed me, starting to make its way up my arm and covering every single cell.

It felt so right. *He* felt so right.

"What the hell is going on?" I whispered again, unsure what to say, what to feel.

I felt him watching me and slowly lifted my head and looked at this stranger... this man I felt like I knew better than I knew myself.

He climbed off Ronnie and turned to face me. I could hear my friend groaning, but I couldn't focus on anything or anyone besides the man in front of me, the man coming close to me. I couldn't move, could only tilt my head back and stare at him. He was so much bigger than me, so much more... masculine than any person I'd ever met in my life.

He was so male.

That was the only word I could think of to describe him.

He started moving toward me, and I was rooted in place, unable to move. The air sawed in and out of my lungs, so forceful I felt like I might pass out.

Finally, I moved backward a step, then another and another until a tree stopped my retreat.

I sucked in a breath as I tipped my head back all the way to look at him.

"What's your name, *my* female?"

My female?

"Rue," I found myself saying. "Rue Franklin." God, I'd just told him my name, that personal information falling from my lips like melted butter from a dish.

"Rue." He said it deeply, his focus on my mouth.

I felt a chill race up my spine at the way he said it, at the way it sounded coming from his mouth. The way his pupils dilated, the fact that his body seemed to get bigger, his muscles more masculine, powerful, had every feminine part of me heating... softening.

"*Mine.*"

And at that lone word that was a deep growl from his mouth, I knew this was the beginning of the end.

And I'd never anticipated anything more.

Chapter Three

Damon

"Rue." I said her name over and over again, the way it sounded turning me on like a motherfucker. "I'm Damon." I wanted her to say my name... scream it out as she came.

A chill raced up my spine, covering my entire body. I wanted to touch her, to see how soft she was, how she felt fully pressed against me.

I looked down at her lips, watched as she licked them, felt my focus becoming unclear as my animal rose up, and I wanted to fuck her right here against the tree. Words spilled from my mouth, whispered low, unintelligible, because I was so fucking lost in this moment.

I'd found her. Finally. She was mine.

I cupped her cheek and smoothed my finger over her flesh. She felt good. Right. Perfect.

"Mate," I said deeply, not stopping myself, not giving either of us any time.

I couldn't stop myself, not when her mouth looked so tempting, so fucking flawless.

Before I knew what was happening or even processed the situation to give her time, I placed my lips right on hers. She gasped against my mouth, and I groaned at her sweet, addictive flavor.

I felt her tense, but only a second passed by before she melted against me. And when I stroked the seam of her mouth with my tongue, all I wanted was for her to surrender to me the way I was for her.

My heart started to jackknife behind my ribs. My bear paced, growled to get out.

She braced her hands on my biceps, her nails digging into my skin. I thought she was going to pull me closer, open wider so I could delve my tongue into her mouth, but instead she gently pushed me back. I had to use a lot of fucking control to pull away, to break that kiss.

And against everything inside me that said to keep her close, I stepped back. I smelled her hesitation, her confusion… that sliver of fear.

But I fucking smelled her pleasure above all else.

I didn't want my mate feeling any of those other things.

She looked over my shoulder at the fucker lying on the ground. I heard him groan and start to stand. But I kept my focus on her.

Always on her.

I watched as she lifted her hand and touched her lips, her gaze unfocused as if she was thinking about it.

"This is insane," she whispered so softly only a shifter with heightened hearing could make the words out. "I have to go," she said, louder this time, and looked at me with wide eyes.

I let her walk past me to the asshole, but before she was out of reach, I grabbed her wrist gently. Sparks of electricity slammed into my body. I heard her gasp and knew she felt it too. We stared into each other's eyes.

"You can run, but I'll always find you." And then I let go of her and watched her and the prick leave. But the entire time, Rue kept glancing back at me, the scent of her lingering arousal filling my head and making me drunk.

Later that night

I PACED MY LIVING ROOM, continuing to stare at my front door, not wanting anything more than to go back to her.

My mate.

My female.

It had taken every single ounce of control, of strength in my body, to leave her. But I'd smelled her hesitation. It had been small, minute in the grand scheme of things.

But it had been there and it instantly had me backing off. Making her feel anything but happiness and pleasure was a no-fucking-go for me.

I should've controlled myself and not beaten the shit out of that little asshole who touched her. It was clear they were friends. But she was my mate.

Mine.

And knowing she was afraid of me, that a fraction of her was uncertain and nervous, made me retreat, giving her space. But I knew her, her name, her scent. There wouldn't be any place on this planet she could run to, could hide from me.

I'd always find her. Always.

I heard someone approaching, their footsteps taking the porch steps two at a time. An involuntary growl left me. I inhaled deeply and scented it was my brother, Oli. I also smelled food.

I was at the front door and pulling it open before he could knock. He stood there staring at me, one eyebrow cocked as he held a covered dish. I knew his mate, India, had made it—a fresh pan of homemade lasagna by the smell of it. I swore my brothers' mates felt sorry for me, always cooking meals, so many that my freezer was filled with Tupperware.

Oli didn't say anything as he held the dish out to me. I made a gruff sound as I took it and stepped back, letting him inside. "Tell India I said thank you. Again. She goes to too much trouble for me." My voice was a low, rough tone, scratchy, because my animal was right there at the surface.

I could feel Oli watching me, and as soon as I glanced up and saw his nostrils flare as he inhaled, I knew he was very aware I was mated. I might not have claimed her yet, but that mating happened, that connection. The scent of it was clear to any shifter.

He narrowed his eyes and a slow grin spread across his face. "About fucking time, brother."

I shut the door and didn't say anything, taking the dish into the kitchen and setting it on the stove. Although the last thing I wanted to do was eat, because—truth be told—I wanted to go to my mate, to make her see she was mine, that I wouldn't back down, I turned on the oven and popped the dish inside. I looked over my shoulder, still seeing Oli smirk.

"Do I keep the aluminum foil on?" You'd think I'd know the answer to such a mundane question, but I was trying to focus on other things, to not talk about this with my brother.

Until I claimed my mate, I didn't want to talk about it with anybody.

Oli shook his head before walking over to the couch and sitting down. "Like you don't have twenty other dishes in your fuckin' freezer right now."

I didn't reply. He grunted at my non-response.

"Leave it in for about fifteen minutes. Then after that, peel the aluminum foil off so the cheese can brown." He didn't look at me as he spoke, and I could feel the frustration coming from him.

He could be annoyed all he wanted. It wasn't like any of my brothers were all about talking about their mates before they claimed them. They'd been grumpy bastards, just like me.

I leaned back against the counter and crossed my arms over my chest, staring at Oli. He did the same to me, his focus trained right on me as if he was waiting for me to tell him everything. I wasn't going to tell him shit though—not because I didn't trust him, but because I didn't want to. I was a selfish fuck when it came to Rue.

He exhaled roughly, as if this whole situation was obnoxious to him, and then lifted his hand to smooth his fingers over his longer hair. After a moment, he stood and faced me, raising a brow as if he knew I wasn't going to budge.

"You stubborn ass." He should know me by now, know that I was just as hardheaded as the rest of them. "Listen, you're mated. I can see it and smell it on you. But I can also tell you obviously didn't complete the claiming. And no doubt that's why you're in this pissy-ass mood." Oli stood and rounded the couch before heading toward the front door. He stopped and looked over at me again. "We've all been there, brother. Give it time. You'll have her, and everything will be exactly how it should be." He nodded once, and I gave a gruff affirmation that I heard him, that I knew what he said was the truth.

But that didn't mean I felt any better about the situation. I watched as my brother left, closing the door behind him, leaving me to wallow in my own self-pity. I told myself there would be no pity, though. There would be no annoyance or sadness or frustration. Because what I was going to do was claim my mate. I was going to make Rue see I wasn't going to stop. I wasn't going to give up, and at the end of it all... she would be mine.

Chapter Four

Rue

I wasn't concentrating on anything but watching the flames dance over the logs. The bonfire my father built with Ronnie was blazing, the heat so intense I didn't even feel the chill in the night air. But I still pulled my jacket closer around me, wrapping my arms around my chest and leaning forward slightly, staring at the fire.

Conversation was going on all around me, our families laughing, beer bottles clanking as they were being pulled out of the cooler. The sound of crackling and popping from the fire filled my head, taking up residence with one consuming thought. One pronounced image.

Him.

Damon.

The bear shifter who said I was his mate. Who said I was his.

This was insane. He was crazy. Yet everything he said felt so… right. It felt perfect and good, like everything I'd been missing in my life. And I'd seen him standing there, looming over Ronnie, violence surrounding him, and all I felt was desire.

I felt this arousal the likes of which I never experienced before. Hell, I'd never actually experienced lust in my life, not unless I was in the privacy of my own home, thinking about some faceless man, a person I didn't even know yet knew better than I did myself.

But as I looked at Damon, that faceless man in my mind had morphed into him. It was like I knew him, like I'd known him for years. I'd touched myself to Damon all these years. He was what I'd been missing.

I wasn't a stranger to shifters. Although I lived in the city three hours away from what they called "bear country," I'd gone to school with lion and wolf shifters. But this was different. This was real, and I didn't want to ignore it, even though I probably should.

"Hey, Rue?"

I blinked a few times and turned to look at Ronnie, who sat on one of the log benches beside me. He held up a beer bottle in my direction, and I smiled and took it gratefully. Maybe some alcohol would do me some good, numb these thoughts and feelings that ran rampant through me.

I brought the beer bottle to my mouth and took a long drink of the hoppy, wheat-tasting alcohol. I didn't much care for the flavor of beer, but then again, maybe a nice buzz would help me ignore all the other stuff currently going on.

"Are you okay?"

I nodded but didn't look at Ronnie after he asked me the question, instead continuing to stare at the flames. Thankfully, he didn't probe, didn't ask me anything else. He left me alone, as did everybody else. They were immersed, consumed in their own conversations, in their own worlds.

I didn't know how long I sat there, but I was now on my third beer, the bottle since warmed from the fire and my hand wrapped around it. Everyone started to get up to go to bed, the moon full in the sky, the flames now dwindling so it was almost pathetic.

"You staying up or heading to bed?" Ronnie asked.

"Probably staying up for a bit. Not too tired right now."

"Do you want me to wait up with you?"

I looked at Ronnie and shook my head. "No. That's okay. I won't stay up much longer." He looked like he might argue with me, offer to stay, even though I really didn't want him to. But thankfully he didn't say anything.

I just wanted to be alone with my feelings and thoughts. Finally, he nodded and stood, giving me a shy smile as he shoved his hands in the front pockets of his jeans and headed toward his tent. I looked back at the flames, at the embers in the burning wood, white and yellow, orange and blue colors dancing along the charred logs.

I heard an owl hooting in the distance, something small scurrying around in the woods. I stood and zipped up my jacket, the autumn night breeze brushing over me and sending a chill along my skin now that I wasn't right in front of the fire.

I stared into the forest, the light from the flames barely penetrating the thick darkness.

I felt this pull, as if something were calling me,

tugging me forward. And then I found myself walking into the forest, not even afraid of the dangerous things that could be lurking in the shadows, hidden behind trees. I swallowed harshly, the thick lump in my throat refusing to go down.

I didn't know how far I walked, but when I looked over my shoulder, the campsite was a good distance away, the dwindling fire like a little speck of light.

I inhaled deeply, still able to smell the smoke from the fire, but also this strong, wonderful wilderness aroma that wrapped around me. It was a mixture of pine, of firewood, fresh air, and freedom. It smelled like a male.

My heart started racing and I turned around, my mouth opening on a silent gasp as my eyes widened. I saw a massive form looming in front of me. And although my eyes had adjusted to the darkness, it wasn't as if I could clearly make out who was in front of me. But I knew. I knew who it was. I knew who he was.

His eyes seemed to glow despite the shadows wrapping around him, and as if my body had a mind of its own, I felt myself warming, becoming wet between my legs, my nipples hardening.

"Mate." He said that lone word on a roughened growl, his voice distorted, sounding inhuman. I knew he was mostly bear, his animal controlling him right now.

"You've been watching me?" My throat was tight, my voice rough. "Stalking me?" I don't know why that turned me on, knowing I'd been thinking of him.

"I make no apologies for watching out for my mate." He took a step closer to me and I refused to move. I was standing my ground, showing him that I wasn't afraid of him or this.

I wasn't. I was aroused.

"You shouldn't be creeping around in the dark watching a woman." God, my voice was so low, barely audible. But I knew he heard me none-theless. "It's weird, right?" I didn't know why I phrased that like a question.

No. It wasn't weird. It felt right. God, it felt so right.

He took another step toward me, and I moved one back. Before I knew what was happening, I was pressed against the tree, just like I'd been earlier today.

"What are you doing?" God, was that my voice?

It was thick, slightly deep, husky, and laced with arousal. I heard it, felt it in my bones.

He said nothing as he crowded me, took up my personal space. But I liked it.

I needed more of it.

Chapter Five

Damon

Fuck. I wanted to take Rue right here and now, pressed up against the tree with the wilderness surrounding us and the only light coming from the moon above us.

I wanted a reckless mating, finally giving my mate my virginity. Taking hers. And I knew she was innocent, untouched. I could smell it, feel it as she looked at me with this uncertainty that screamed vulnerability.

She was mine. She'd only ever be mine.

"This is fast. Too fast," she said breathlessly. I heard the need in her voice, the way her words were nothing but a lie.

This wasn't too fast. We both needed more.

She was wet. I smelled it too, could practically taste that sweetness in the air.

I didn't stop myself from leaning in and running the tip of my nose up the length of her neck. I all but purred out in pleasure as she tipped her head to the side and gave me better access, a soft moan spilling from her.

"That's it, my mate. Surrender to me." My words were barely a whisper with how worked up I was, how much I needed to slip my hand between her legs and see how wet I made her. But I didn't want to rush her. I wanted her to be completely ready to give herself over to me. Because when that moment happened, it would be sweet bliss. Nirvana.

So against my better judgment, against my bear roaring out that I was making a big fucking mistake, I inhaled deeply by her neck once more before pulling back. She had her head resting on the bark of the tree, her eyes closed, and her lips parted slightly. My mouth watered to taste her again, to kiss her.

"Look at me," I demanded harshly. And when she opened her eyes and stared at me, everything so clear, so focused, I knew only death would keep me from her.

Kiss her. Take her.

I cupped the side of her throat and slammed my mouth down on hers, taking her lips in a brutal, possessive kiss. I couldn't stop myself, couldn't control anything that was going on.

I expected her to push me away, maybe even slap my face. But she moaned, wrapped her arms around my biceps, and pulled me in closer. It was as if she couldn't help herself. Maybe she couldn't. Maybe she was just as far gone as I was.

And although I knew she felt this pull, the connection mates had with each other, she was also human. She wouldn't feel what I felt, the intensity. She wouldn't know how it was for a shifter to find their fated mate.

But she would. I'd make sure of it.

I'd show her, tell her, make her feel that she was the only one for me... forever. She would know the only thing I wanted in my life was to make her happy, to please her. Hell, I wanted to feed her from my hand.

I leaned, grinding my erection against her belly. The fucker between my thighs was thick and hard, long and incessant. I could feel my pants starting to get damp from how much pre-cum seeped from the tip.

"Tell me what you want." I knew I shouldn't have demanded it, should've gone easy with her, but I couldn't help it where she was concerned.

I'd waited for her my entire life, and now that she was here, it was like this flood was moving through my body, drowning everything with need and possessiveness and passion.

I continued to thrust myself against her like some obscene fucker, but my bear was doing most of the actions right now. He was feral and intense.

"This is so... crazy," she whispered, her warm breath teasing the side of my face. "Not telling you the truth seems wrong."

I knew what she meant. It was the mating pull, her need to be completely honest with me, to give me what she wanted as much as what I wanted.

"Tell me," I growled.

She started breathing harder, heavier. "I want this. You."

That's all I wanted to hear. That's all I'd ever wanted to hear. I leaned back and stared into her face. I cupped each side of her neck, my thumbs smoothing across her cheeks as I stared down at her lips. And then I slammed my mouth down on hers.

I kissed her with all the pent-up arousal and passion I had for her, all the desire and lust that had been building up in my very marrow for my entire existence.

We kissed for what seemed like an eternity and I never wanted it to end. I never once stopped grinding myself against her, the front of my jeans damp from all the pre-cum that spilled from the tip of my cock. I smelled her arousal, the wetness between her thighs. It was like spun sugar coating the air.

So fucking sweet.

She broke the kiss and panted, and I wanted to fucking take her mouth once more.

"We should slow down. This is so new to me… no matter how right it feels."

Yes, so fucking right.

"You want slow?" She nodded in response. "I'll give you all the time you need. You control the reins, baby girl." She gasped a little at my endearment. I smoothed my finger along her bottom lip and she parted her mouth. "I'm not going to be far, Rue. Never."

And then I left, giving her space, giving her time. But I meant what I said.

I would always be close. Always.

Chapter Six

Rue

"Are you sure you don't want me to wait for you?"

I glanced over at Ronnie and shook my head. He looked so concerned at the moment. It would've been comical if I didn't know how serious he was.

"No, I'll be fine. Being alone would be kind of nice." I looked around at the wilderness that surrounded us. "I kind of like it out here. It's peaceful."

"Listen," he said, and I glanced back at him. I could tell he was nervous, and I had an idea of where this was going. "I know things have been weird recently, and I know you said how you feel, or don't feel, about me." He ran his hands up and down his jean-covered thighs, glancing around as our families finished packing up the campsite. "But I wanted to know if you think you and I have even a small chance of giving it a go?" He looked at me so hopefully, and I knew I had to clear things up.

I thought about Damon, his face coming to mind. I looked at Ronnie, the bruise he had on his cheek angry-looking. I thought about the way we'd played it off like he tripped and hit his face on a rock. We didn't talk about why he got his ass kicked, hadn't even discussed with each other what Damon said to me. To be honest, I didn't even know if Ronnie heard all the things Damon said, how I was his mate, how he would not let me go.

But the truth was it didn't even matter. I wasn't going to stop feeling these things toward Damon. I couldn't. The very idea of ignoring them seemed abhorrent, so wrong in nature that they made me physically ill.

Ronnie was my friend, had been for a long time. But the feelings he had for me clouded his judgment. I knew that. I needed to clear things up now —again—or things would only get worse.

"Ronnie, I know the feelings you have for me go

beyond being... friends." I swallowed the thick lump in my throat, because this felt awkward. "But I don't feel those things for you." And then I looked at him, a little bit nervous about what he'd say. I'd spoken only loud enough so he could hear.

I didn't know what I expected. Maybe for him to be upset. Disappointed. I was prepared for just about anything, anything aside from him acting like it was no big deal.

"Yeah, I figured. But I wanted to give it one more shot." He gave me a sincere smile, and I felt as if the stress was off my shoulders. "It's about that man in the woods, right? The shifter?"

I was nervous all of a sudden at hearing his words. And then I nodded, unable to stop myself, knowing he was right, that what I felt was real, that this was all about Damon. "Yeah."

He nodded. "I kind of heard what he was talking about right after he kicked my ass." He chuckled a little bit and lifted his hand to his bruised cheek. "I've never actually seen a mated shifter before." He shrugged. "But I guess what they say is true about them being possessive."

I didn't know what to say to that, so I just kept my mouth shut.

We were kind of in this limbo, not saying

anything, awkwardness between us. But I think it was just on my end, because Ronnie seemed easygoing at the moment, like this wasn't bothering him.

"Can you guys give us a hand?" Ronnie's dad hollered out, and it snapped my attention into focus.

We moved into action, cleaning up the campsite and packing everything in the cars.

Twenty minutes later, I stood there and waved at my family driving away then did the same for Ronnie's until it was just Ronnie and me standing there, his car to my left, mine to my right.

"Are you sure you don't want me to hang back with you?"

I looked at him and smiled, shaking my head. "I'm sure. But thank you." There were a few moments of silence, and then he finally nodded.

"Have a safe trip back and send me a text when you're home so I know you got there, okay?"

I smiled again and nodded. "Okay." I inhaled deeply as he started making his way toward his car, but before he got in, I called out to him. "Ronnie?" He stopped and looked over his shoulder. "I'm really sorry about everything. I'm sorry about you getting hurt. I'm sorry about things not happening between us." I thought saying this again out loud would've been weird, but it felt natural. "I guess I'm just sorry about a lot of things."

He faced me and gave me a genuine smile. "The only thing I want is for you to be happy."

Ronnie was such a good guy, and I knew he'd find someone who deserved him. And I was sorry I wasn't that person, because Ronnie was a catch and he'd make some girl very happy one day.

He got into his car and I watched him leave, lifting my hand and waving goodbye. I stood there for a few moments, and when I couldn't see his car any longer, I closed my eyes and breathed out slowly. Several seconds passed as the wind whistled through the leaves on the branches that surrounded me.

"I know you're there," I said and opened my eyes, turning around slowly. I saw Damon standing between two thick oaks, his body seeming just as big as those trunks, just as sturdy and strong. Powerful.

He had on a flannel shirt that molded to his impressive body, the worn jeans he wore fitting him perfectly. His body was big but lean, his muscles defined like a swimmer's. I instantly felt myself heat, become aroused. But this wasn't just about desire. The feelings I had were much stronger, more pure and genuine. I felt connected to him, as if I'd known him forever, as if I'd been searching for him my entire life and hadn't actually realized it.

I saw a flash of gold in his eyes and knew his bear was right there. I found myself taking a step closer, then another and another, until we were only a few feet apart now, until I could smell the cologne he wore—or maybe it was his natural scent, a smell that had my heart racing and my body lighting up.

I didn't know what to say, what to do next. In my heart, I knew what I wanted, and that was him. Damon. My bear-shifting mate. But logically, I knew this was fast, intense. Was it reality?

He took a step toward me and I held my breath. "It's reality. Truth. It's our reality." He ate up the distance in a few long, stealthy strides, and when he was right in front of me, I tipped my head back and looked into his dark eyes. He had a day's worth of scruff covering his jaw and cheeks, this masculine appearance that made me so feel so very feminine. All I could feel, hear, smell… was Damon. And I wanted more. I wanted so much more I wanted to breathe it.

I wanted to live it.

The words were right on the tip of my tongue, words I never thought I'd utter to a man, let alone one I didn't even know. But I did know him. I felt like Damon had been a part of my life for as long as I could remember, this faceless presence in my fantasies, in my desires and wants and needs.

Say the words. Tell him what you've wanted to say for your entire life.

Those words played over and over in my head, and the whole time he just watched me, as if waiting for me to speak them, as if he knew what I wanted to say. I took a deep breath in, taking his very essence into my lungs, into my body, and letting it become imprinted, ingrained in every single inch of me.

As I stared into his dark eyes, knowing how this would end, knowing our fates were intertwined, that we were now forever a part of each other, I knew what I wanted to do. I knew who I wanted.

"I want you, Damon. I need you now."

Chapter Seven

Damon

And here we were, in my cabin, the lights low, a fire started. When she told me she wanted me, there had been no stopping my actions. When she told me she needed me now, I had her in my arms in seconds flat. I had her in my cabin before either of us could even think this through.

But there was nothing to think about. We were meant to be together. We were supposed to be together always.

I pulled Rue close to me, standing in my living room, the fire crackling beside us, the scent of her desire filling my head and making me feel drunk.

She was sweet and so fucking soft against me. And when Rue touched my arm, curled her nails into my flesh, my cock jerked like it had a mind of its own. And I guess it did. I was a fucking virgin, never having even gotten off, because all I wanted was my mate.

The first time I came would be when I was buried inside of Rue's tight pussy.

I wanted her, wanted to have her in my bed and claim her. I wanted my mark on her, my young growing inside her. I growled low, wanting her to admit she was mine.

No one will ever have you but me, Rue. No one.

The tether of control in me broke, and I grabbed the back of her head at the same time I slammed my mouth down on hers and stroked her tongue with mine. She gasped against my mouth, and I swallowed it whole, taking it into me. I started walking us backward, the primal side of me rising up and screaming out to take her, my bear demanding to take this further.

I groaned into her mouth, my cock hard, demanding. She placed her hands on my chest and pushed me back. And as hard as it was, I retreated. I didn't want to, but for her, I'd do anything. She controlled me.

I stared at her face; Rue's cheeks flushed, her mouth parted, and her lips were glossy. She seemed high, her eyes half-mast as she looked up at me. I was at the point where my animal wanted to come out and devour her, shove my cock deep in her pussy, and fill her with my seed.

"Damon." She breathed out my name and it sounded so fucking good. "Your eyes." I watched as her throat worked when she swallowed. "Your canines."

"My animal, mate. He's coming out for you, because of you." I stared at her lips again. "He wants you, Rue."

I knew what I looked like, knew my body was changing because of my need for her. I was changing. I made a low, animalistic sound in the back of my throat and moved closer to her. She didn't retreat as I placed a hand on either side of her head, caging her in, leaning in farther so our faces were only inches apart. Closing my eyes and inhaling deeply, I smelled her arousal. But she wasn't afraid of these feelings, of her need for me.

She was wet between her thighs... for me.

I stared right in her eyes and moved one of my hands closer to her face so I could run my thumb along the shell of her ear. "I'll never hurt you, will never let anyone else hurt you." I could barely breathe. "I'll always protect you, see you're cared for, but never underestimate what a mated male will do, the lengths he'll go for his female." I leaned in another inch until our lips were close enough so that when I spoke they'd brush together.

"That's… intense."

I growled in approval.

"There isn't anything or anyone who will take you from me. Ever." I closed my eyes again and inhaled. "I can smell how wet that virgin pussy is for me." I couldn't stop the low sound that left me.

For long moments, she said nothing, but then she swallowed once more and opened her mouth to speak. "I'm not some piece of property you can just claim," she said softly. "I'm human. This isn't my world." The way she spoke was so low only a shifter would hear.

I LOOKED DOWN at her lips. "This is your world now, baby. You're my world." I lifted my gaze to her face again. "And make no mistake in thinking you can run from me. Ever." I ran my finger along the side of her throat, her pulse beating wildly beneath her ear. "Your scent, Rue… your scent is ingrained in my very cells." I growled the words out, unable to stop myself. "I'll find you anywhere, *my* female. There isn't any place on this fucking planet you'll be able to hide from me."

I heard her gasp and ground my hard cock against her belly. I knew she felt how hard I was, could smell her arousal thicken in the air.

"Damon," she whispered.

"You feel that?" I asked, but she didn't respond, just licked her lips. I bared my teeth so she could see how my canines had lengthened, how my bear was coming out. "I'm going to claim you, Rue. I'm going to take your virginity and give you mine. I'm going to shove my cock so far into you, you won't know where I end and you begin." My cock jerked at that, at the image I saw in my head. Her eyes widened farther. I leaned close so my mouth was by her ear now. "And I'll use my canines, let my bear out even more to pierce this pretty throat of yours, to mark you so everyone knows you're mine."

She was breathing harder, faster, and the scent of her arousal rushed into me, turning me on impossibly more.

I leaned back so I could look into her eyes again then placed my hand right over her belly. We hadn't even had sex, but I could already picture so much with her.

"My babies will be growing in here, in you, Rue." I added a little bit of pressure on her stomach. "Every single fucking time I take you, I'll fill you up, my goal to get you big and swollen with my young, to claim you from the inside out."

This little sound left her, one of shock but also sexual need. Longing.

I watched her chest rise and fall. "You may not fully understand, Rue, but you will. This is your world now, and you're mine."

Chapter Eight

Damon

I wanted her.

I need her.

She looked at me, her eyes wide. "I want you, Damon." The sound she made had every part of me tightening.

My fucking cock jerked and I ground my teeth to try to control myself. I knew I had to sample my female now. The scent of her lust rose, and I felt my body become tighter, ready to finally claim the one woman who was meant to be mine and mine alone.

"Rue, baby, when I first saw you, my animal, my entire fucking world, came alive." I inhaled deeply again, taking in her scent, her essence into my body.

"I knew you would be mine even before I knew what you looked like, who you were."

I crouched in front of her, both of us only inches away now, breathing the same air, experiencing the same electricity and arousal... the same pull. I smoothed my finger over her bottom lip and felt her tremble for me.

"There isn't anyone or anything that will keep me from you, that will take you from me."

"I want that, too," she said low, soft. She reached out, curled her hands around my biceps, and pulled me closer. For long seconds, we just looked into each other's eyes, and I had a hell of a time not taking her right then and there, fiercely and possessively, rough and fast.

I smelled her nervousness, her innocence, and I knew I needed to take this slow with her, or as slow as I could make myself.

"You'll only ever be mine. No other male will have you." I leaned back and inhaled deeply, so drunk off the smell and sight of her. I couldn't handle it. "You'll never know what it feels like to have any cock but mine." She made a small sound of need for me. "You'll never know the feeling of a male's hands on you but mine, Rue baby." I looked into her eyes, knowing she could sense how serious I was. How could she not when I was growling the words in a purely bear way?

She breathed harder, faster, and I allowed my inner animal to come forth, willingly letting him have his time in the sun without having to push my human side out of the way. We could share this moment.

"Now," I said and heard the deepness, the distortion in my voice. "Let me see how you look bared, Rue. Let me see what's mine."

She swallowed, and after a moment passed, she gave me what I wanted. She gave it all to me.

I couldn't help but breathe hard and fast. I wanted her; that was undeniable.

She looked at my mouth and then back at my face. "I'm nervous, Damon."

I closed my eyes and groaned. God. She sounded so sweet. So good. "I know. But there's no need, baby. Trust me to make things good for you, to be gentle and thorough."

I had her up in my arms seconds later, turned, and walked us over to my bedroom, right to my massive bed.

Once she was lying on her back, her hair fanned out over the white sheets, I just stared at her.

The sight of her was a visual orgasm. I took a step back and admired the view.

I stood there for long moments just staring at her, and then in a gruff voice I said, "Open for me, mate. Let me see what I'll be claiming, marking tonight."

She opened her thighs for me, her pussy now on clear display, and a harsh groan left me. I was on my knees before her seconds later, the animal in me demanding I claim Rue, take my mate in all the ways a bear shifter does with his fated female.

I smoothed my hands up her legs, over her thighs, and curled my fingers into her soft flesh. I pulled her thighs apart even farther and leaned in until there was only an inch separating our mouths. My denim-covered cock was pressed against her inner thigh.

"God. Damon," she whispered, her mouth brushing against mine as she spoke.

"You want me, don't you?"

She nodded. "I want this—you—so badly."

I leaned back and looked down at her gorgeous chest, her breasts rising and falling almost violently with her increased nerves and arousal. My mouth watered for a taste.

I looked at her face, gauging her reaction, seeing the ecstasy on it.

"Damon," she moaned.

I loved it when she said my name. "How wet are you for me, Rue?"

She breathed out slowly. "I'm so wet for you."

I hummed in approval. "And this is all for me, isn't it?"

She nodded.

"No. Say the words."

"It's all for you, Damon."

"That's right it fucking is, baby girl." I made another low, pleased sound in the back of my throat. I slipped my hand between her legs while still staring at her. But I didn't touch her pussy right away, just kept my fingers poised right on her inner thigh, right by that crease where her leg met the tight, hot little part of her. The heat from her pussy could have scorched me. But fuck, I wanted to get burned.

Pulling her leg even farther out with my other hand, I didn't deny either of us. Not anymore.

I touched her pussy.

She opened her mouth and gasped, and I wanted to swallow that sound, take it into my body.

I spread my fingers through her wet, soaked slit and grunted in arousal, in pleasure.

"Damn, baby. You're so ready for me."

"God, Damon," she whispered.

"Not God, mate. But you'll be screaming that by the time I'm done with you."

Chapter Nine

Rue

God, this was really happening, wasn't it?

Am I really doing this?

Were we really doing this?

He tangled his fingers in my hair, winding his big hands in the strands and claiming my mouth again. For long moments, we kissed, our moans matching in intensity. He finally pulled back, and I sucked in a lungful of air.

"You ready for me, *mate*?"

I nodded. "So ready, Damon."

He leaned back, this dark, aroused look covering his face and turning me on even more.

Damon gazed down the length of my body, looking his fill and making me feel like there was no other woman in the world for him. And I knew there wasn't.

"I need you." I didn't even hesitate as I said those words. This moment was perfect, exactly what I wanted, what I needed.

He lifted his gaze from between my thighs and stared into my eyes. "I'm going to make you feel so fucking good you can't walk straight tomorrow, female," he spoke low.

A shiver worked its way up my spine.

Damon leaned closer so he had his mouth by my ear now. "You'll be weak-kneed, because you'll still feel my cock deep inside you."

The dark, delicious words had my pussy clenching. "Yes."

"You primed for me?" he asked on a whisper.

I didn't even lie. "Yes."

Damon wrapped his fingers around the column of my neck, adding just the smallest amount of pressure. He didn't leave his hand there for long before he smoothed it back down my chest and settled it right between my breasts.

And when he leaned in, I felt his lips along my

jaw, loving the stubble from his cheek as it slightly abraded my flesh. Inhaling deeply, I took in his intoxicating scent, the aroma that made him all male. I absorbed the pleasure moving through me. I lived in this moment.

He moved his mouth along my neck, stroked my skin with his tongue, and God, did it feel so good. I knew he could be so rough with me, just take what he wanted, but he made sure this was good for me too.

He moved his mouth back to my ear and whispered, "Are you ready for me, female? Ready for me to take your virginity and give you mine?"

I shivered in response, unable to help myself. "I'm ready," I actually managed to say. "I've been ready for you my entire life."

His erection pressed against my inner thigh, so big and long, hard and massive. "That's right, you have. Just as I have been for you."

We gazed at each other for a moment, neither speaking, but our breathing was loud, identical.

Damon gazed down at my mouth. Then his lips were on mine and his tongue speared between them. He tasted potent, powerful.

Male.

"You'll own me just as much as I own you, mate."

He gently bit my lip, and a gasp left me. A fresh gush of moisture left my pussy.

I had my hands on his chest, his muscles firm beneath my palms. God, he was so strong. He growled out, grabbed my wrists in a firm but gentle hold, and brought my arms above my head. I was stretched out for him like an offering, but maybe that's what he wanted.

The growl that came from him was gruff, so dangerous-sounding that I should have been afraid, not impossibly wetter. He leaned down and ran his tongue along the arch of my throat, which had me moaning out for more, not even caring that I begged him.

And then I was flipped onto my belly with my ass all but in the air. I felt him smooth his hand down the length of my spine. My heart was beating in my throat and I heard it in my ears. Sweat covered me, these little beads that seemed to turn me on even more.

Everything was happening so fast, but I didn't dare stop it, not for how inflamed I was.

He ground his erection against my ass, and I closed my eyes and bit my lip until the pain gave way to the coppery flavor of blood on my tongue. He was huge.

My pussy clenched at the thought of him shoving all of that inside of me.

I looked over my shoulder to see him getting undressed, watching in awe as he revealed all that hard, golden flesh. And then there was his cock.

God. He was big.

He grabbed himself and started stroking his dick.

"You like what you see, Rue?"

I nodded but didn't actually say the words.

"Yeah, you do," he said as if he were pleased. "This is all for you." He took a step closer. "This will only ever be for you."

My throat tightened, my mouth going dry.

And then Damon was back on top of me a second later, his naked erection now on my ass. A gasp left me at the heat that came from him, at the feeling of his pre-cum smearing along my over-heated flesh.

This felt good, and he wasn't even inside me yet.

He placed his hands on either side of my outer thighs, slowly moving them up. His hands were warm and big, making me feel every inch a woman.

They were real man hands, ones that knew what it meant to work hard.

He groaned. "I can smell how much you want me, mate. I can smell how sweet your pussy is, how wet and ready for me."He pressed his dick into the crease of my ass. "Fuck, your ass is perfect, nice and round, like a fucking peach." He leaned in so his lips were by my ear. "And I fucking love peaches, baby." His words were low, and he squeezed his fingers on my thighs again. "I'll make this good for you, be gentle this first time, Rue."

Damon moved down the length of my body until I felt his warm breath along the top of my ass. He kissed and licked my flesh and then grabbed the cheeks and clenched his fingers around the mounds. When he spread my bottom and the cool air moved along the crease, I let out the breath I hadn't known I'd been holding.

He groaned, and I knew he was staring at the area he'd exposed. "You're so fucking juicy for me." He speared a finger through my slit. "Ask me for it again, mate."

"Please," I begged, unashamed.

Damon spanked my right cheek first, the sound of flesh being hit echoing off the walls. I'd never thought this would turn me on, but it seemed everything Damon did had that effect.

"Your body craves me, knows I'm the only one who can ever sate it." He rubbed me between my legs again, proving I was even wetter after he spanked me.

At the first touch of his tongue on my pussy, I couldn't contain the cry that left me. And then he feasted on me like I was his last meal. Damon licked up the center of my pussy, and I cried out from the pain and pleasure coalescing into one.

"*Yes.*"

He groaned against me, the sloppy sounds of him eating me out filling the room.

I clenched the sheets beneath me, needing something to hold on to. I shifted slightly, my ass ending up being propped up more, obscenely shoved in Damon's face.

"Yeah, that's so fucking it, baby." He licked at my pussy harder, faster, sucking my clit into the hot, wet depths of his mouth. That was the end of it for me. I came for Damon.

When the tremors in my body stopped, Damon pulled back but wasn't nearly done with me, apparently. He pushed my legs open more, and before I could contemplate what was happening, he had me flat on my back again. He bent down between my thighs and had his mouth right back on my pussy.

Damon was relentless as he rubbed my clit, moving that thick digit around the opening of my body, not penetrating me but promising he could take me any way he wanted. And I yearned for that.

"You want me inside?"

I nodded, unable to find my voice.

He started to penetrate me with his finger, just one, and very slowly. Damon wasn't harsh or demanding. He took his time, making me beg for more. For him.

And then he had his mouth on my clit once more. I didn't know how much I could take.

The sound of his voice made vibrations on my clit, and I moaned out for more.

He murmured incoherent things against my flesh. But I heard one thing clear as day: "Mine." He started sucking especially hard on the little nub, and I came again for him.

When my pleasure receded, we were both panting harshly.

I closed my eyes, breathing in his scent, that dark, intoxicating aroma. It felt so good to have him hold me, to have his big arms wrapped around me, making me feel protected and cared for. When I opened my eyes again, it was to see Damon staring down at me.

I took a moment to just look at him, at the way his body was so big and powerful, how I imagined he could crush anything that stood in his way. I felt myself become even wetter, desperately wanting him inside me. I watched as his pupils dilated, a dangerous aura surrounding him.

"Rue," Damon said softly, with heat. He inhaled, his nostrils flaring slightly, and a tingle spread through me at the knowledge he was taking in the fact that I was wet for him, that I wanted him desperately. This low, animalistic sound left him. He had his head lowered, running the tip of his nose up the length of my throat. I couldn't help but close my eyes again.

"I can smell how much you want me, *mate*," he said in a deep whisper.

He cupped my cheeks in his big hands, leaned back, and looked into my eyes. I felt his calluses, this masculine feeling that had my inner muscles clenching.

Warmth spread through me.

He lowered his gaze to my mouth. Damon moved his hands down my face, stroked his fingers along the sides of my neck, and continued lower until he gripped my hips. I didn't know if I'd stopped breathing or was hyperventilating in that moment. Everything was a blur of ecstasy.

He kissed me while he did this, stroking his tongue over my lips before delving it into my mouth. He flexed and released his fingers on my hips, and I knew this mating would cement every single thing I knew about the world, about my life.

The fire running through my veins could not be ignored, could not be extinguished, and I didn't want it any other way.

He broke the kiss and started moving his mouth down my neck, stopping at my collarbone. "So. Fucking. Sweet."

I breathed out heavily, because at the moment, it was all I could do. Damon made me wet and so ready to take him into my body. I felt like I was losing all control.

A shiver worked its way through me, and I didn't stop myself from grabbing his head, tangling my fingers in his short dark hair, and pulling his head back until I could look into his eyes.

His nostrils flared slightly, his mouth parting from desire. I took control of the kiss now, giving back just as fiercely as Damon had. He groaned against my mouth and grabbed a chunk of my hair, pulling the strands until pain mixed with the pleasure.

After long seconds, he finally broke the kiss.

I moaned in disappointment, but then when he ran his tongue back down my neck and along my pulse, that disappointment turned into pleasure.

"I'm going to mark you so fucking good."

He was rock-hard, so big and thick that wetness coated my inner thighs. He smoothed his hands over my ass, down the back of my thighs, and gripped behind my knees. Before I knew what was happening, Damon had his hand between my thighs once more. It didn't matter how much he touched me, how many times I got off... I felt like I needed more.

"Damon," I said and closed my eyes as his big fingers found my soaking slit. I wrapped my thighs around his waist. He claimed my mouth once more, and speared his tongue between my lips.

I moaned and grabbed on to his shoulders for support. Our breathing mingled, and for that moment, we were one.

"We're perfect for each other, Rue." The way he murmured those words against my lips nearly had me getting off.

I shivered at his possessive demeanor. "Yes. Yes we are."

My gaze drifted farther south, leading to what I wanted most at the moment.

Yeah, I was going to move this along, going to actually give my virginity to my bear-shifting mate. Because not doing this wasn't an option.

Chapter Ten

Damon

Fuck, Rue was all mine.

Mine.

I was trying to rein in my desire for her, to go slow, make this sweet and soft, gentle. But fuck, I couldn't.

Her naked body called to me in the most primal of ways. I heard her swallow, saw the slender line of her throat work up and down.

"My mate…" My throat was fucking tight, dry. "I could try to have my fill of you, but I'd never be sated." I lifted her head with my finger under her chin, forcing her to look at me.

When Rue licked her lips, I was riveted to the

sight, imagining her mouth wrapped around my cock. Fuck, I was an obscene fucker. I reached out and pushed a piece of her hair from her forehead. "Tell me you're mine," I whispered.

Without any hesitation, she said, "I'm yours."

That pleased me so fucking much. It pleased me so much I actually growled from it.

I smoothed my hands along the bare flesh of her shoulders, continued down her arms, and then stopped at her waist.

"I'm only yours," she moaned.

I leaned in farther and moved my tongue along the seam of her lips. Her flavor was addictive, exploding along my taste buds. And when she started kissing me back, I didn't stop the groan that left me. I forced myself to break the kiss and trailed my lips along her jawline to her ear. "I am so hard for you, Rue. So fucking hard for you all I want to do is fill you with my seed."

She made this soft noise, one that sounded like need and desperation and everything that turned me on. I slipped my hand behind her nape, curled my fingers into her soft, warm flesh, and started kissing her pulse, which beat rapidly beneath her ear. I pulled her closer so I felt her breasts press to my chest. Hell, I swore I felt her heart beating against mine. A low growl left me, one I couldn't stop.

I kissed her neck and nipped her lightly, my canines aching to pierce her flesh. "I'll make you feel so fucking good. Always."

"Yes," she murmured. Rue dug her nails into my body, and the sting of pain mixed with my desire. My cock jerked.

I knew I had to claim her now. I'd been trying to go slow, easy, and make her see I could be gentle and give her the time she needed. She held the cards, pulled the strings, but right now, I was fighting with my desire and primal need to make her mine irrevocably.

I dragged my hand up her belly and over her ribcage to cup one of her breasts. I thrust my pelvis forward, grinding my cock into her softness, unable to stop myself from groaning.

I sucked at her neck, dragged my tongue up the slender column of her throat, and thrust back and forth against her softness, grinding myself against her, because I was so fucking horny for her. I let my canines run over her soft, fragile human flesh, my mouth watering to taste her, to puncture her skin and mark her.

Pulling back was hard as hell, but I managed to

do it, to breathe in deeply. I looked down at her body then moved back up, memorizing every part of her, and finally stopped at her breasts once more.

I was going to devour her.

I wrapped my hand around the nape of her neck, pulled her forward, and lowered my head to lick the curve of her throat from collarbone to ear. Damn, her flesh was sweet, addictive.

Mine.

She gasped and moaned out, "That feels so good."

My cock grew harder at her admission. I took hold of her nipples between my thumbs and forefingers, pulled at the already taut flesh, and listened to her groan in pleasure. I was shaking with the force to keep calm. And when I lowered my head, removed my hands, and sucked at one of her turgid nipples, she pushed her chest farther into my mouth. After a few seconds, I let go of her nipple with an audible pop, stared at the pebbled peak, and saw how red and wet it was.

My dick was so hard it ached, and my balls were drawn up tight to my body, ready to fill her up with cum. Right now, all I wanted to do was attack her like the animal I was, to fuck her hard and rough, just like my bear wanted me to.

I parted her legs with my hands on her knees and forced her to become obscenely wide for me. And then I stared at her pink, wet center, her pussy a work of fucking art. I felt like I could snap right then and there.

I need to go slow, to be gentle.

When I took hold of my dick and started stroking myself from root to tip, unable to control my need to touch myself as I looked at her, I felt copious amounts of pre-cum line the tip. My seed covered my palm, and I used it as lubrication.

I was so fucking close to coming, my balls filled to the max with my need for Rue.

"Touch yourself. Do it for me. Let me see how much you can please yourself." And that was the last thing I said before I stood back and waited for her to do just that.

Rue

There was no way I was going to deny him, to deny me. I touched myself, showed him the most intimate part of myself, my virgin pussy. I wanted to please him, wanted to make Damon desire me as much as I wanted him.

I looked down at the long, thick length of his cock. It stood hard between his muscular thighs, pointing right at me, the slit at the tip glossy from his pre-cum. God, he was so… masculine. All male.

"You like what you see, female?"

I nodded instantly.

Damon stroked himself in slow, lazy motions, his focus on me.

"Say it."

Even more clear fluid dotted the tip of his cock from his arousal, and I finally lifted my gaze from his impressive length to look at his face. "I like what I see," I whispered.

He took a step closer until he was at the edge of the bed and kept his gaze trained between my splayed thighs. On instinct, I started to close them.

"No, Rue. You keep those fucking pretty thighs open for me."

God. Yes.

His muscular chest clenched as if he couldn't contain himself, couldn't control himself. He stroked his cock a little faster, the sound of his palm moving over his flesh filling my head in an obscene auditory orgasm. His bicep contracted and relaxed from the rapid motion of him jerking off.

"What do you want?"

"You," I cried out in pleasure.

Damon stroked himself a couple more times before groaning and moving onto the bed with me once more. He placed his hands beside my hips, and I felt myself grow wetter at how big he was hovering over me, at how powerful he looked.

The way he watched me made me feel desire like I'd never felt before. I realized Damon was the only man I'd ever wanted, the only male I'd ever want.

"Tonight… tonight, I finally claim you, and finally I'll know what my mate feels like, how tight you are when I thrust my cock deep in you and fill you with my cum." He sounded so fierce, so sure of everything right now.

He didn't make me wait long before he claimed my mouth, forcing me to take all of him. And God, did I want that, did I want all of him. His flavor was sweet and spicy. I couldn't help but make this small noise in the back of my throat, this sound of pleasure. I wasn't able to stop myself. But it was as if that small sound was his breaking point. He snapped. I felt his bear rise up, could feel that animal push forward.

He moved his hand behind my head to cup it, tangled his fingers in my hair, and forced my head back. My throat was now arched, bared for him. He broke the kiss and panted. I felt the hot, hard length of his cock press between my thighs as he kissed my neck, licking the skin. I wanted to feel him stretching me, pushing into my body until I ached, making me feel full and complete... owned.

"So good, Rue. You feel so good." He reached between our bodies and placed the tip of his cock at the entrance of my pussy. I gasped involuntarily. Everything inside me stilled, tensed, and I panted with anticipation, with excitement. He pulled back, looked into my face, and the fierceness that covered his expression made me picture his animal right in front of me, baring his canines, showing me how fierce he really was.

"What do you want?" I whispered.

He growled low. "You. Only you. And I'm taking what belongs to me, my female."

I licked my lips compulsively.

"So are you ready for me, mate? All of me?"

I nodded, unable to actually say the words.

As he stared at me, he pushed into me in one fluid motion, causing my back to arch and my breasts to thrust out in need. He claimed me, my virginity, my innocence. He groaned above me, his eyes closed, his body taut. I felt the heavy weight of his balls press against my ass when he was fully inside me. He stilled, and I knew he was letting me adjust to his size, his thickness. I felt full, stretched, and the discomfort was so shocking that I couldn't catch my breath.

When he started moving in and out of me, faster and harder with each passing second, I reached out and grabbed onto his biceps, digging my nails into his firm, warm flesh. He breathed hard, heavy, keeping his eyes closed.

Sweat covered his face and slid down his temples, turning me on even more. His massive chest rose and fell as he breathed, as he tried to control himself.

"Damon. I need you."

"Fuck," he said harshly. He pushed into me and pulled out, over and over, groaning with every thrust.

I felt my inner muscles clench rhythmically around his thickness, and we both grunted in pleasure.

"Rue, mate, watch as I claim you."

I gasped slightly. When the tip of his cock was lodged in the opening of my body once more, I rose up and braced my elbows on the mattress, wanting to watch him as much as he wanted me to see what he did to me... watch as he fucked me.

I stared between my thighs, where I could see his massive dick shoved inside me. And when Damon started to pull out, I could see how wet his length was from how soaked my pussy was.

"So fucking tight, Rue. God, you're so fucking primed for me."

He moved in and out of me slowly, making love to me, sweat dripping down his temples and his chest. With each passing second, he picked up speed until he was slamming his dick into me, and all I could do was curl my nails into his biceps and hang on.

"Yes," I moaned and let myself fall back on the bed, closing my eyes and opening my mouth as I felt ecstasy consume me. He went primal on me then, the sound of our wet skin slapping together filling the room, making it so that was all I heard.

"I need to feel you get off for me, Rue. I need it."

Right before I felt myself falling over the edge,

Damon pulled out of me and flipped me onto my belly.

A gasp left me at the sudden feeling of emptiness and at the quick movement, but Damon didn't make me wait long to feel full, to be stretched once more. He palmed my ass with his big hands, gripped the mounds, and squeezed them tightly until I moaned from the pleasure and pain.

"So fucking perfect. You are so fucking perfect." He grabbed my waist and hauled me up so I was now on my hands and knees. He was so rough, so alpha. I looked over my shoulder and saw him lean back, watched as he stared between my legs, where my pussy was on display.

I felt him place the tip of his cock at my entrance once more and I bit my lip. And then he was sliding into me in one smooth, fluid motion.

I gasped.

"Yes," I whispered.

Damon thrust in and out of me slowly, but as the seconds moved by, I felt him picking up his speed, his intensity consuming me. He growled and held on to my hips in a bruising hold. *Yes*. I wanted his marks on me.

"Watch. Look."

I looked down the length of my body, where I

could see the heavy weight of his balls swinging as he thrust in and out of me. A silent cry left me, and I closed my eyes as pleasure washed through me.

He groaned, and my pleasure increased. "Mine," he grunted out.

Damon held on to my hips so tight the pain had me gasping and my eyes widening. He buried himself deep inside me, stretching me, having me feel every damn thick inch of his dick.

"Fuck," he roared out, and I felt the hard jets of his cum fill me. "Rue," he roared again and had his mouth at my throat. I felt him pierce my throat, the pain mixing with pleasure.

He filled me with his seed until all I could feel, smell, and hear was Damon, was his bear claiming me.

It was long moments later when he pulled his mouth away and breathed out harshly. "This is just the beginning."

I nodded, knowing that was the truth.

He covered my back with his chest, his breath coming out in hard pants. That warm, humid feeling covered my flesh, calming me. My arms shook as I held myself up, the pleasure consuming me. When Damon pulled out of me, I couldn't help but collapse onto the mattress. It was only a second later when Damon was lying beside me, his arm over my waist, his hand sliding down between my thighs. He gathered the cum that slipped out of me, and pushed it back into my body.

"My cum belongs in you, Rue." He moved his hand from between my legs and pulled me in close to him once more. Our skin was sweaty, damp from fucking, his cum filling my body, my pussy sore in the best of ways. I'd never felt more content than I did in that moment.

"Rue. *Christ*, baby. My female," he said huskily against the side of my throat.

This warm feeling consumed me when he kissed the top of my head. I closed my eyes and sighed. He pulled the blankets over us, and I leaned closer, snuggling in and loving the heat that came from Damon.

I inhaled deeply, taking his scent into my lungs, and couldn't help but smile. I felt safe, protected in Damon's arms. This had never been my world, but God it was now. It felt like I was always meant to be here. With him.

This all felt right, and I didn't want to let that go.

I wouldn't.

Chapter Eleven

Rue

I felt a little intimidated and very anxious as I stood in Damon's living room and greeted each of his brothers and their mates. There were only five brothers, so it should've been easy enough for me to remember their names, but I felt like everything that was said was going in one ear and out the other, my nervousness so pronounced my hands were actually shaking.

And then I felt Damon wrap his arm around my waist, pulling me in close, giving me that support I needed. I tipped my head back and looked into his face, seeing he already watched me, a smile spread across his lips, his warm brown eyes showing me without words that he loved me more than anything else.

Although this mating had been fast and hectic, unexpected, it felt so right. It felt like this was exactly where I was supposed to be, wrapped up in his arms and meeting his family. And later today, he'd be formally introduced to mine.

After introductions were made, with genuine happiness from Damon's brothers and their mates in welcoming me, we all started preparing dinner. It was like a family affair, all of us working together.

Mena and Cason were making the dessert, Maddix and Allison were preparing the homemade apple cider, and Ainsley and Asher were finishing off the fresh bread with honey spread. Bethany and Zakari were having a loving, teasing argument on how much butter to put in a specific recipe. And then there was Oli and India working on setting the table, Oli whispering things in India's ear that had her blushing.

All I could do was stand back with a glass of warmed apple cider Allison had given me and smile, feeling like I already belonged in this family unit. And the children... God, the children were adorable and sweet, kind and rambunctious. I could see the brothers in each of them, little snippets of their personality coming out.

I hadn't come from a big family, no siblings, only one aunt and uncle on either side, and the fact that I felt like I had an instant family with these bear shifters and their mates had this perpetual grin spread across my face.

I took a sip of the cider, the liquid warm and spicy, with hints of nutmeg and cinnamon dancing across my tongue. I looked over at Allison and said, "Delicious." She grinned and tipped her glass in my direction before taking a long drink.

I felt strong, big arms wrap around my waist, pulling me back toward an equally powerful chest. I instantly smelled Damon, the scent of the wilderness that surrounded us mixed with the spicy aroma that was all him.

"Missed you."

I grinned at his words and turned my head to look up at him. "You just had me an hour ago," I whispered so only he could hear. My cheeks felt hot as I blushed, remembering how he'd pinned me to the wall in the home we shared and fucked me until I came three times.

He slipped his hand down to cover my belly, his

mouth by my ear. "When should we tell them about the little one inside you?"

I felt my face get hotter, pleasure and happiness filling me.

"It's so early."

He hummed and kissed the shell of my ear. "They'll be able to scent you're pregnant before too long, mate."

I knew this, but I liked just us knowing. I hadn't known Damon would be able to smell me being pregnant before I even knew, but apparently a shifter could smell their mate carrying their young before any other shifter even suspected.

"You're right," he said low and against my ear. "I like having this little secret between us, at least for the time being. But the truth is, I also like the idea of everyone knowing you're carrying my baby." He kissed my temple.

I leaned back and sipped my cider, enjoying watching everyone interacting so naturally, so lovingly. This was what I'd always wanted.

This was what we both deserved.

Epilogue

Damon

Five years later

I stoked the fire and stared at the flames. The scent of the meal we just had lingered in the air, filling the cabin. My mate had fed me well, cooked the buck I'd gotten for us earlier this week and made a delicious stew out of some of the meat, as well as homemade peach cobbler. My female was one hell of a cook.

I looked over my shoulder at the couch where Rue sat, a book in her lap and a blanket thrown over her feet. I loved watching her read, loved knowing she was in her element when she got lost in her books.

She was gorgeous when she was like that.

The years had gone by in a blur of wonderful, happy memories. I protected what was mine, making sure Rue and our children were safe and cared for above all else. They were the reason I lived now, the reason I did… everything.

I looked down at my mate, pushed her long hair off her face, and felt my chest tighten at the emotions that filled me every time I looked at her. My mate. My better half. My everything.

She was the mother of my son, of my daughter that was growing in her belly. She was the reason I breathed every day. Pushing down my bear, because the bastard wanted her more and more each day, I slid my hand under the blanket and placed my hand over her swollen belly. She was due with our little girl in a month, and I couldn't help the smile that spread across my face.

I felt our baby girl kick.

Rue ran her hand over my bicep, and for long seconds we just lay there in silence. "You ready for another one?" she asked softly.

"Mate, I've never been readier for all of this. I love you."

"I love you too." She rose up and kissed me back.

I rubbed my hand over her belly for several long minutes. "Although it'll be hard to keep the little fuckers away from her when she's older. I'm gonna want to keep her under lock and key."

Rue started chuckling. "Yeah, figured you would be like that. So protective." She snuggled in closer to me.

I felt my daughter kick again and knew I'd protect what was mine at all costs.

Every day, I loved Rue more. She was my mate, my wife, the very reason I breathed. I'd die for her. I'd kill for her.

"Are you happy?" I asked her this constantly, wanting to hear her say it. It pleased me.

"You make me so happy, happier than I could have ever dreamed of, mate."

Fuck, I loved hearing her call me her mate.

"Are you happy?" she asked softly.

"*You* make me happy, Rue. You and our family. Our life."

She leaned forward and pressed her lips to mine. "I love you, Damon." I groaned as her lips brushed along mine. "I love you so much."

I cupped the back of her head and pulled her an inch closer. For long seconds, I just kissed her, pleased when she melted against me. "You're my life, baby girl."

She sighed, and it was that small sound, that little act, that had pleasure filling me.

I moved my hand to the side of her throat so I covered the mark I'd given her during our first mating. Rue was my female, my mate.

Mine.

I ran my thumb along the mark on her neck. I fucking loved looking at it, loved knowing I gave it to her… that she was mine.

I pulled her closer and just held her, loving how soft and warm she was, how pliant she was in my arms. She was mine forever, and nothing would take that away. It had been years since I'd found her, claimed her as a proper mate did, and every day I fell in love with her, connected with her more than the last.

She was my mate, the mother of my young, and the female I was meant to be with from the day I was born. I felt that consume every part of me.

"Momma."

The sound of Ayden had Rue and me sitting up.

She held her arms out to our son. "Come here, sweetheart. Come lay next to Momma."

I pulled the blanket down and smiled as he ran up to our big bed and climbed up, his little body struggling a second before he finally got on top.

Ayden snuggled between us and I pulled the blanket over us, kissing him on top of the head then leaning in and kissing Rue on the lips softly.

I stared at Rue and listened to her softly hum to Ayden, lulling him to sleep.

These lives were my world, and nothing and no one would ever change that.

I drifted off to sleep with my family beside me, my hand on Rue's belly and the world at my feet. This was what it meant to truly survive, to really be happy and live.

I hadn't known what that was, felt what it was like until she'd come into my word, until we had our little family.

She made me who I was.

And I was never letting go.

The End.

IT STARTED WITH A
Kiss

AND ENDED WITH HER BEING MINE

USA TODAY BESTSELLING AUTHOR
JENIKA SNOW

IT STARTED WITH A KISS

By Jenika Snow

www.JenikaSnow.com

Jenika_Snow@Yahoo.com

Photographer: Wander Aguiar

Cover Model: Dane DeBruin

Image provided by: Wander Book Club

Cover design by: Designs by Dana

Editor: Kasi Alexander

Content Editor: Kayla Robichaux

piracy of copyrighted materials that would violate the author's rights.

IT STARTED WITH A
Kiss
AND ENDED WITH HER BEING MINE

Ari

It was supposed to be a fun, easygoing bachelorette party. But it turned out to be so much more.

They dared me to kiss the next guy to buy me a drink. And I agreed. It was just a kiss, right?

And then it happened... I saw Grey and felt something instant.

I tried to back out of that kiss even though I wanted it desperately.

But he didn't let me stop it. He kissed me until my toes curled and my heart raced. He kissed me until I knew I wanted more.

So when I left him standing there staring at me, I knew it was all kinds of wrong to leave.

Grey

It started with a dare.
It ended with a kiss.

And for weeks after she walked out of my life, I searched for her, doing anything and everything in my power to find a morsel of information about the first woman to make my heart stop and my future flash before my eyes.

And when I finally found her, I was going to show Ari that I'd known she was mine from the very beginning.

And that I wasn't letting her go a second time.

Chapter One

Ari

"Shot. Shot. Shot. Shot."

I tried to tune out the three already heavily intoxicated women shouting in my ear like they were at a frat party.

I lifted up the tiny glass and eyed the colored liquor inside. My stomach already clenched in queasiness.

"Don't bitch out now, Ari."

I narrowed my eyes at Francesca, or Franny as we called her, the bride-to-be and resident instigator of our little group.

"You can't be sober at a bachelorette party,"

Bernadette said. "I think that's some kind of sin or something."

"Yeah, no party poopers tonight," Kai responded, then promptly giggled.

I snorted. "One of us should keep a clear head, right?"

The girls booed, and I glanced around, giving sympathetic looks to everyone around us. We were being loud, they were drunk, and no doubt the people around us thought we were a bunch of idiots.

But when I looked at Franny and saw what a good time she was having, I said fuck it. Let them be loud. Let us be obnoxious. And for once in my life—at least for tonight—I was hanging up my literal librarian persona and letting loose.

I tossed the shot back and the girls clapped and cheered. The alcohol burned down my throat, settling in my stomach so it felt like a lead ball. I wheezed and coughed, my eyes watering, and reached for a glass of water. After I sucked that down, I was reminded why I didn't really drink. It made my face red, I was one hell of a lightweight, and my hangovers were pretty horrendous.

But this was a once in a while type of thing,

celebrating with my friend before she got married, so what's the worst that could happen?

"What's new in the dating world with you?" Franny asked and picked up her beer, taking a long drink from it as she watched me over the rim, expectant of my answer.

I shook my head, not even wanting to go there. "What dating world?"

"Girl," Franny said and started laughing. "We need to get you out there so you can get that V card punched."

I rolled my eyes at her library reference.

I might be a librarian, but even I found it corny.

"Yeah, we need to get that V card punched real good."

I glanced around, Franny's drunkenness making her especially loud. A few guys looked over at us, one grinning and the other wagging his eyebrows.

Yeah. Hard no, boys.

I might have been a virgin, have the whole tight bun and schoolteacher look going on, but I wasn't so desperate to get rid of my virginity that I'd give it away to some drunken asshole.

"Oh my God," Lizzie said, her eyes wide as she looked between us. "I have the best idea." She was already three sheets to the wind and there was no stopping or slowing her down. None of them.

"By the look on your face, I can see it's a really bad idea," I said and leaned back against the chair, afraid to hear this.

"Ari, to make things fun, spice it up, I dare you to kiss the next guy who buys you a drink."

I was shaking my head before she even finished talking. "Nope. I'll get some gross asshole. That would be my luck." I looked at the guys who'd been eyeing me after overhearing the whole V card conversation with Franny.

They were grinning at me.

I internally cringed.

"Come on," Bernadette pleaded. "Not like you'll ever see them again. It's all in good fun."

"Besides, you're never able to let loose. Tonight is the first time in what, like forever that you let your hair down? Literally." Franny held up her shot glass and grinned.

"What they said," Kai said and hiccupped.

I was going to say no again, but as I looked at my three best friends, saw them grinning and pleading, I knew they were right, that I didn't let loose, that most times I did have a stick up my ass. It had been forever since I let myself enjoy just being out... just being alive.

It was just a kiss, right? But under no circumstance was I going to accept a drink from the creepers sitting at the table beside us who'd overheard the conversation.

"Okay, fine," I said, and the girls started clapping even louder. "I can handle a kiss from a stranger, but I reserve the right to turn him down."

The girls started shaking their heads. "Nope, a dare is a dare."

"What if he's like sixty?"

Franny shrugged. "Does the saying about getting better with age count toward dick too?"

I nearly spit out the water I'd been about to swallow.

"Come on. One kiss to the next guy who buys you a drink," Bernadette and Kai said in unison.

I exhaled and sat back in my chair. "Fine. I accept the challenge."

About the Author

Want more of the Bear Clan? Find them here:

https://amzn.to/2HY5jNF

Want to read more by Jenika Snow? Find all her titles here:

http://jenikasnow.com/bookshelf/

Find the author at:

www.JenikaSnow.com
Jenika_Snow@yahoo.com